THE STONE

A PERSIAN LEGEND OF THE MAGI

Dianne Hofmeyr

Pictures by Jude Daly

FARRAR, STRAUS AND GIROUX

For my father, who taught me to be a stargazer ~ D.H.

For Lara Joy and Jess ~ J.D.

Source Note

In 1296, Marco Polo was imprisoned for two years in Genoa, where he dictated
an account of his travels, including the story of the Magi of Saveh, to a fellow prisoner,
a Pisan scribe called Rustichello. Various versions were copied into Latin and have been
translated into many languages. This retelling is based on versions described in *Marco Polo*
by Richard Humble (Putnam, 1975); *The Travels of Marco Polo—a Modern Translation* by
Teresa Waugh (Facts on File, 1984); and William Dalrymple's *In Xanadu: A Quest* (Vintage, 1990).

Text copyright © 1998 by Dianne Hofmeyr. Pictures copyright © 1998 by Jude Daly
By arrangement with The Inkman, Cape Town, South Africa
All rights reserved
First published in Great Britain by Frances Lincoln Limited, 1998
Printed in Hong Kong
First American edition, 1998

Library of Congress Cataloging-in-Publication Data

Hofmeyr, Dianne.
      The stone: a Persian legend of the magi / Dianne Hofmeyr ; pictures
by Jude Daly. — 1st American ed.
            p.   cm.
      Summary: A retelling of the story told to Marco Polo about the
Magi of Saveh, three wise men from a town in Persia, who follow a
strange star and find a special child.
      ISBN 0-374-37198-9
      1. Magi—Legends. [1. Magi—Legends.   2. Folklore—Iran.]
I. Daly, Jude, ill.   II. Title.
PZ8.1.H72115St   1998
398.2′0935′01—dc21   97-46038

In the year 1271, seventeen-year-old Marco Polo boarded his father's galley and sailed out of the lagoons of Venice into the open sea. It was the start of a journey that took him across the Mediterranean, through Arabia and Persia, over the Great Salt Desert, across the highest mountains in the world and on to China and the magnificent court of the Kublai Khan, ruler of the mighty Mongol empire.

On his way, Marco Polo stopped in Jerusalem at the Church of the Holy Sepulchre, where he was shown a lamp that had burned continuously for over 1,200 years. Marco Polo took some oil from the lamp as a gift for the Kublai Khan.

When he passed through the town of Saveh, in Persia, he came across three strange, ornate tombs with domed roofs. The people of Saveh told Marco Polo that the names of the three men buried in the tombs were Balthasar, Melchior and Jasper, and this is the story they went on to relate...

Across the wind-swept plains of Persia, in the ancient town of Saveh, stood a tower...a tower encrusted with turquoise tiles and filled with strange instruments, mysterious charts and glowing flasks of potions.

Each starry night, three men climbed to the top of the tower to explore the heavens through narrow stargazing tubes.

T hen they bent over their charts and plotted the positions of the
stars they had seen. The people of Saveh believed the stargazers
were magicians, but Jasper and Melchior and Balthasar were more
than that: they were also healers and holy men.

One evening, as the sky darkened, a star like no other star appeared in the west. It filled the sky with brilliant trails of fiery light.

"A new planet! We've discovered a new planet!" shouted Jasper, as he caught the dazzling movement in his stargazing tube.

"No, no!" Melchior pointed upwards. "Look at the trails. It can only be a comet."

Balthasar shook his head and measured its place in the heavens. "It's a mystery. We must consult our charts and scrolls."

They spent days searching feverishly through scrolls and rolls of scribblings. At last they came across a strange legend, telling of a baby whose birth would be announced by a star. The baby was a king who would bring justice and healing and peace to the world.

"We must find the child and honor him," said Balthasar.

"Let's take him a gift of gold," said Jasper. "If he's a king, he will gladly accept gold."

"If he's a healer," said Melchior, "he will be pleased with ointment of myrrh."

Balthasar shook his head. "We must give him a gift of holy incense. If he accepts incense, then he is a true holy man and will bring peace."

So they set off across the desert, following the route of the merchants, to find the child. Each man carried a gift, carefully wrapped, in his saddlebag.

During the day, when scorching winds sent dust devils whirling into the air, they rested in the shadow of their tent, eating dates and drinking dark, bitter-herb tea.

By night, they journeyed under a sky that tossed out its milky pattern of stars like a flying carpet.

And all the while the brilliant star shimmered and swept across the heavens just ahead of them.

At last the star stood still. Beneath it, they saw a simple shelter.

Jasper wanted to be first to present his gift. He jumped down from
his camel and rushed into the shelter. But when he saw who was inside,
he forgot about his gift and ran out, wide-eyed with excitement.

"He's not a child. He's a young man, like me!"

"That cannot be," said Melchior, and pushing past him, he entered
the shelter. But he, too, came out quickly.

"How strange. He's middle-aged, like me!"

Last of all, it was Balthasar's turn. But when he came out, he shook his head. "You are both wrong. He is old, like me."

"He can't be young, middle-aged *and* old!" said Jasper.

"How can he seem different to each one of us?" asked Melchior.

"It's a mystery. Let us go in and offer our gifts together," said Balthasar.

So Jasper, Melchior and Balthasar went into the shelter together. And they found that they had all been wrong. There before them was a young child with his mother.

For a moment they stood in silence. Then they knelt down and laid their gifts in front of him.

The young boy smiled and accepted all three. Then he held out a small sealed box.

"This is my gift," he said.

Jasper stepped forward and clasped it tightly against his chest.

In silence, they climbed onto their camels and journeyed back to Saveh. But Jasper felt the weight of the unopened gift in his saddlebag. He grew impatient. Finally he cried, "Let's open it! Let me break the seal."

But Balthasar shook his head. "Be patient. Wait until we reach the tower."

At long last they came to a well where merchants from the far corners of the earth had gathered to water their camels. The camels were loaded with spices and silks and dark-dyed indigo cloth, cornelians and rubies the color of pomegranate seeds, glowing amber, brilliant blue beads of lapis lazuli and rich tapestries.

Yet all Jasper, Melchior and Balthasar carried was the small, sealed box that Jasper clutched.

"What is in your box?" one of the merchants asked.

"It's a gift," said Jasper proudly.

"What kind of gift?" asked the merchant.

Jasper held the box to his ear and shook it gently. "I don't know."

"Why don't you have a look?" said the merchant. "Perhaps it's gold."

Jasper's fingers rubbed at the seal.

"Yes!" he said. "Yes, I will open it." And before Balthasar or
Melchior could stop him, he broke the wax and lifted the lid.

"A *stone*!" he cried. "It's only a stone!"

"Is that all?" said the merchant, and he spat a trail of date pips
into the sand in disgust.

Melchior turned to Balthasar. "Why did he give us a stone?" he asked. "It must mean something."

"The stone holds a mystery," answered Balthasar.

"It's a useless stone!" Jasper cried. "We can't even trade with it!" And jumping up, he flung it down the well.

Melchior watched it fall. "But why did he take our gifts and give us only a stone in return?"

"Ahhh…now I see!" said Balthasar.

"What? What do you see?" asked Jasper, peering down into the darkness of the well.

Balthasar's eyes shone. "The child accepted all three of our gifts. He must be all three things."

"What three things?" demanded Jasper.

"The true king. The true healer. And the true holy one."

As Balthasar spoke, flames of fire suddenly shot from the well, and a great blaze of light filled the sky.

The merchants came running out from the shadows of their tents. "What is happening?" they asked, shielding their eyes from the brilliance.

"It is our gift from the child," Balthasar announced. "A gift that will bring justice and healing and peace into the world. Our belief in this must be as strong as the stone and burn in us like fire."

Wide-eyed, the merchants stared into the brightness.

"Come!" cried Balthasar. "Come and share this. The gift is for everyone!"

So, one by one, the merchants came forward and held their lamps high to be lit by the fiery light.

Then each person carried the flame away, back to all the faraway places
of the earth, for all mankind to share.